GO FETCH!

GROSSET & DUNLAP
Penguin Young Readers Group
An Imprint of Penguin Random House LLC

Library of Congress Cataloging-in-Publication Data is available.

Part of Boxed Set ISBN 9781101950654 10 9 8 7 6 5 4 3 2 1

MAGIC BONE

GO FETCH!

by Nancy Krulik
illustrated by Sebastien Braun

Grosset & Dunlap
An Imprint of Penguin Random House

For Ian, my DC connection!—NK

For Graham—SB

CHAPTER 1

"Throw the ball, Josh!" I bark. "Throw the ball!"

My two-leg, Josh, is holding a ball in his paw. He looks straight ahead and gets ready to throw.

My tail is wagging back and forth. It loves playing fetch.

My paws are bouncing up and down. They love playing fetch, too.

"Throw the ball!" I bark. "Throw the ball."

Josh doesn't speak dog. But I think he knows what I'm saying because he throws the ball.

"I got it! I got it!" I bark excitedly.

My paws run after the ball. Fast. Faster. *Fastest.*

Fur flies into my eyes. It's hard for me to see. But my paws keep running. Fast. Faster . . .

Crash! Ouch! I bang right into the tree in my yard. Stupid tree. Stupid fur in my eyes.

I look up and see a girl two-leg. She's standing by my tree holding the ball in her paw. *My* ball. Who is this two-leg? And why did she catch my ball?

Now *she's* throwing my ball in the air.

Yay! The girl two-leg wants to play!

"I got it! I got it!" I bark.

My paws bounce up high in the air. My mouth opens wide. "I got it!" I bark again.

Chomp! I grab the ball in my mouth. I run over to Josh and drop it at his feet.

Josh picks up the ball. He shakes his head and says, "No, Sparky. No!"

Sparky, no? I've heard those words

before. But usually it's when I grab some food from the table. Or drink from the big white water bowl Josh uses when he has to make a yellow puddle.

Josh never tells me *no* when we're playing fetch. *Until now.*

Josh throws the ball to the girl two-leg. She fetches it and throws the ball back to him. No one is letting me fetch the ball.

No fair!

I watch as the ball goes back and forth between Josh and the two-leg girl.

Finally, Josh drops the ball on the ground. My tail picks up. My ears stop drooping. My paws start *boinging*.

Anything on the ground is mine! That's the rule.

Wiggle, waggle, woo-hoo! It's my turn to play with Josh!

I fetch the ball and start to run. But before I can reach him, Josh and the girl leave the yard. Then I hear a loud noise. It's Josh's big metal machine with four round paws.

The machine sounds like it's going away. But, that's okay. I can play fetch by myself.

I spit the ball out of my mouth. It doesn't go very far. This game of fetch isn't any fun.

What now? I know! I race over to Josh's flower bed and start *diggety, dig, digging*. *Diggety, dig, dig. Diggety, dig* . . . WOW!

It's a bone. A bright, beautiful, sparkly bone.

Sniff, sniff, sniff. It smells so good. Like chicken, beef, and sausage all rolled into one.

"Hello, bone!" I bark excitedly.

The bone doesn't bark back. Bones don't bark.

This bone smells so meaty. I just have to take a bite . . .

Chomp!

Wiggle, waggle, whew. I feel dizzy—like my insides are spinning all around—but my outsides are standing still. Stars are twinkling in front of my eyes—even though it's daytime! All around me I smell food—fried chicken, salmon, roast beef. But there isn't any food in sight.

Kaboom! Kaboom! Kaboom!

CHAPTER 2

The *kabooming* stops.

I look around. I'm definitely not in my yard anymore. I'm in a big park. It's full of trees and two-legs. And there's a gigantic water bowl running right through it.

What's going on? How did I get here?

Wait a minute. I know how I got here. The bone. It *kaboomed* me to . . . well . . . wherever I am.

It isn't just any bone. It is a *magic* bone. I've taken bites out of it before. And every time, I've ended up somewhere else.

Like the day my magic bone took me to London and I ate chips. Which are really fries.

Or the time it *kaboomed* me to Hawaii and I ate shave ice.

And the time my magic bone sent me to Rome and I ate meatballs. Which were almost as *yummy, yum, yum* as the cheese I ate when I *kaboomed* all the way to Switzerland.

I wonder what food I will find here.

I wonder where *here* is.

Rumble, rumble, grumble. My tummy is hungry. I can tell because I speak tummy. *Rumble, rumble, grumble* means "feed me!"

But first I have to bury my bone in a safe place. This bone is the only thing that can *kaboom* me back to Josh's yard when I want to go home.

That is, if I decide that I *want* to go home. I'm not sure Josh needs me anymore. He has a new friend now. He plays fetch with her. And he takes her for rides in his metal machine with the four round paws. I wonder if she likes sticking her head out the window like I do.

I spot a tree with lots and lots of flowers on its branches. I'll bury my bone right near the tree. That way I can find my hiding spot when it's time to dig up my bone and go home. *If* I go home.

I start to *diggety, dig, dig*. Dirt flies everywhere.

I've made a big hole. I drop my bone in, and push the dirt right back over it. Now my bone is completely hidden. No one will ever find it—except me, of course!

Wow. All that *diggety, dig, digging* has tired me out. I sure would like to curl up on Josh's lap and take a nap.

But Josh went away and took his lap with him.

Still, there are plenty of two-legs around here. Maybe one of them would like to have a sheepdog puppy curl up in his lap.

Aha! There's a very tall two-leg sitting on a chair inside a big white building. His lap looks huge.

I run to the building. I dash up the stairs.

Two-legs leap to the side as I climb the stairs. They don't want to get in my way. What nice two-legs!

Up, up, *uh-oh*!

That sure is a big two-leg sitting in the chair. I don't know if I can jump all the way up into his lap. But I'm gonna try.

Boing! Boing! My paws bounce up and down as I try to jump high enough to reach the tall two-leg's lap.

I can't.

So I'm just going to curl up at his feet. Maybe he will bend down and pet me, like Josh does when I curl up at *his* feet.

Aaahhhh. The floor feels so cool against my belly.

"Okay, big two-leg," I bark. "Pet me!"

But the two-leg doesn't bend down to stroke my fur. He doesn't move at all. That's when I realize that the giant two-leg isn't a *real* two-leg. He's a statue.

I know all about statues. I saw lots of them when I was in Rome. Statues look like two-legs, but they're made of stone.

Still, there are plenty of real, live two-legs around here. And they're all pointing at me and yelling.

I don't like when two-legs yell at me. It's loud. And scary.

Quickly, I run down the big white stairs.

Suddenly, a two-leg runs toward me. He looks angry.

What if he's a dogcatcher? They grab dogs and put them in the pound. I know. I got thrown in a pound in London. There was no dirt to dig up and no windows. I don't want to go to a pound ever again.

Run faster! I tell my paws.

My paws *zoom, zoom, zoom* until finally they stop behind a big green bush.

Phew. There are no two-legs around anywhere.

I don't have to be scared anymore. There's no one hiding here in the bushes but me!

Achoo!

Uh-oh. What was that?

Achoo!

Someone's coming. Someone I don't know. Someone who might not like dogs.

I've got to find a better place to hide. And quickly!

CHAPTER 3

Before I have the chance to move, I come face-to-face with a terrier.

Achoo! He sneezes.

"Who are you?" I ask him.

"Aren't you going to say *bless you*?" the terrier asks me.

"Is that something dogs say to each other in this place?" I wonder aloud.

"It's something you say *any*place when someone sneezes," the terrier replies. "Not just here in Washington, DC."

Washington, DC. That must be the name of this place.

Achoo! The terrier sneezes again. He wipes his nose with his paw.

"Bless you," I say this time. "You sure sneeze a lot."

"It's the cherry blossoms," the terrier tells me. "There are a lot of them this time of year. I'm allergic."

"Hi, Allergic." I sniff his butt to say hello. "My name's Sparky."

"What?" the terrier asks. Then he starts to laugh. "No, my *name's*

not Allergic. My name's Fala. I just meant that something in the cherry blossoms makes me sneeze."

"Cherry blossoms?" I ask.

"Those pink flowers up in the tree," he tells me. *Achoo.* "I hate 'em." *Achoo.*

"Bless you," I say.

"You're new to Washington, huh?" Fala asks me.

"Yeah," I answer. "I just *kaboomed* here."

"You just what?" Fala asks. Then he sneezes. *Achoo!*

Oops. I almost told Fala about my magic bone, and I'm not sure I want to do that. I don't know Fala at all. What if he's the kind of dog who steals other dogs' bones?

"Bless you," I say again.

"Thank you. Where are you from?" Fala asks me.

"Josh's house," I reply.

"Josh is your two-leg?" Fala asks.

I don't know how to answer that. Josh was my two-leg. And he still might be. But he might not be. He might have found someone else!

"I used to have a whole family of two-legs," Fala says before I have a chance to answer. "But I got tired of being stuck home all the time when they went away. So one morning I bolted out of the yard. I've been on my own ever since."

Wow. Fala's story sounds like what happened to me. "Don't you miss them?" I ask Fala.

Achoo! "Nah," Fala says between sneezes. *Achoo!* "Now I'm never bored. There's always something exciting going on in Washington. And I'm in the middle of it, instead of being cooped up in the yard."

"How long have you been on your own?" I ask him.

"For lots of dinners and breakfasts," he answers.

Grumble. Rumble. As soon as my ears hear *dinner* and *breakfast*, my tummy starts talking.

"Are there good scraps in Washington?" I ask.

"Yes, the yummiest!" Fala tells me. "Pretzel pieces, hot-dog buns, bits of ice-cream cone."

"I love ice cream!" I tell Fala.

"Then come on, Sparkster," Fala tells me. "Let's go have some scraps!"

Sparkster? I don't like that name. It's not what Josh calls me.

But Josh isn't here. Fala is. He's the only friend I have in Washington. So I don't say anything. I don't want to make Fala angry.

"Hurry up," Fala says. "It's picnic time on the Mall."

"The Mall?" I ask him as we run.

"Yeah," Fala says. "Two-legs call this park the National Mall. I call it my food bowl."

Achoo! Fala sneezes and snaps up a piece of pretzel. I see another piece of pretzel lying on the ground. Fala doesn't notice it. He's too busy staring at a chubby two-leg sitting on

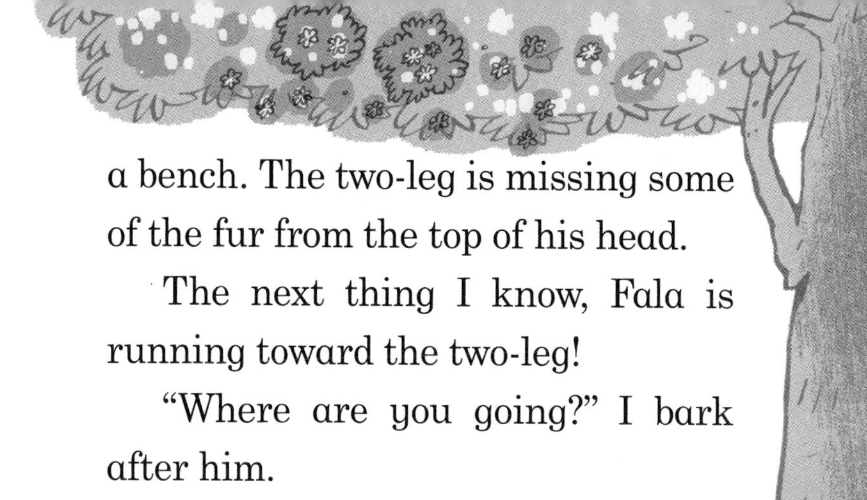

a bench. The two-leg is missing some of the fur from the top of his head.

The next thing I know, Fala is running toward the two-leg!

"Where are you going?" I bark after him.

Fala doesn't answer. He just keeps running toward the bench.

I watch as Fala walks over and sniffs at the two-leg. The two-leg jumps up, surprised. He moves away.

Fala pads back to me. He looks sad.

"Who was that two-leg?" I ask him.

"N-nobody," Fala says. "I thought it was someone I knew. But it wasn't." *Achoo.* He sneezes again and wipes his nose with his paw.

I nose the piece of pretzel on the ground. "Are you going to eat that?"

Fala shakes his head. "Nah. You take it, Sparkster. There's plenty of food around here."

Fala points his snout toward a family of two-legs. They're sitting on the ground eating chicken.

Wiggle, waggle, woo-hoo! The food is on the ground. That means it's for dogs! I run right over.

But before I can grab a piece of chicken, I see something fly by. It's a ball! A small two-leg just threw it to a big two-leg.

They're playing fetch!

"Can I play, too?" I bark as I run for the ball.

The two-legs don't understand what I'm saying. So I show them. I jump up in the air and catch the ball in my teeth. Then I bring it over to the young two-leg.

The young two-leg looks at the ball. He looks at me. Then he yells and starts to run away.

I think he's scared. I don't know

why. I'm not scary. I'm just a puppy. Puppies are *never* scary.

But big two-legs can be scary. Especially if they're angry.

"Sparkster, we should get out of here!" Fala calls as the angry big two-leg starts to come near us.

Fala takes off.

And since I don't want to get yelled at anymore, I take off, too—right behind my new friend.

CHAPTER 4

Thumpety, thump, thump. My heart is thumping so hard.

Stop thumping, I tell my heart.

Fala and I stop near the edge of the giant water bowl. I stick my head in and lap up some of the cold water.

"You're pretty fast, Sparkster," Fala says. "I'm glad. For a minute there I wasn't sure we were going to get away without being caught."

Gulp. "Caught?" I ask nervously.

Achoo. Fala sneezes. Then he frowns. "We're supposed to be on leashes when we're on the National Mall," he tells me. "It's a dumb rule. And it's not really fair to dogs like us who are living on our own."

On our own? Fala was right. I used to be with Josh. Now I'm on my own.

Well, it doesn't matter right now. I'm sure there are lots of things to do here. Like over there—there's a giant white stick. It's standing straight up. It's so tall it looks like it's touching those white fluffy things in the sky.

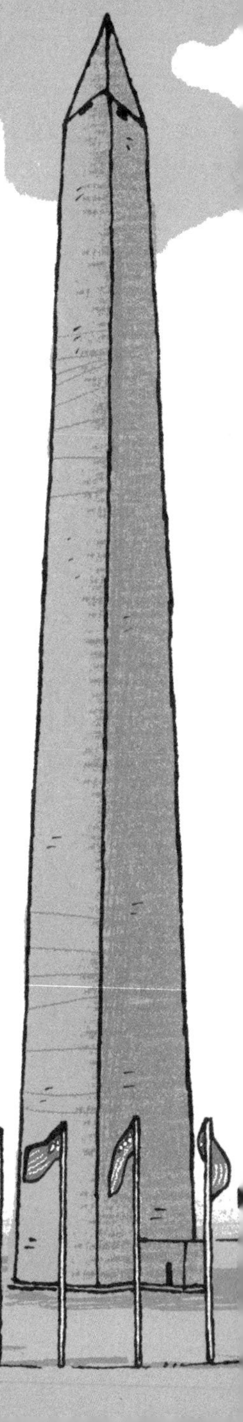

"That's the biggest stick I've ever seen!" I tell Fala. "I don't even think my friend Frankie could fetch that stick. And he's a big German shepherd."

Achoo. Fala sneezes and shakes his head. "That's no stick," he tells me. "That's the Washington Monument. It's made of stone. From the top, you can see all over the city."

"All over?" I ask him.

"Uh-huh," Fala tells me. "They don't let dogs up there. But I've snuck up a few times. I can sneak you up there, too!"

I'm not sure we should go up to the top of that Washington Monument stick. It's pretty tall.

But I don't want Fala to know

I'm scared. I want him to think I'm brave. Just like him.

"Let's go!" I try to sound excited.

Fala runs off toward a crowd of two-legs.

Before I can follow Fala, I have to stop at a tree. I need to get rid of some of the water I just drank.

As I lift my leg, I notice a piece of paper stuck to the tree trunk. There's a picture of a dog on the paper. And not just any dog.

"Hey, Fala!" I bark. "The dog in that picture looks like you."

But Fala can't hear me. He's already near a crowd of two-legs. I hurry to catch up to him.

Fala is sneaking around the two-legs. They don't even notice him.

MISSING
Fala

But I'm bigger than Fala. I keep bumping into their legs.

"Ouch!" I bark as a two-leg steps on my paw.

The two-leg jumps. He stares at me with his mouth open. Then he quickly moves away.

"Hurry, Sparky. Catch up!" Fala barks as he enters a building.

Fala is running into a room. I run in there, too.

"Okay, Sparkster, here we go!"

Fala says as the door to the room closes.

"Go?" I ask him.

Uh-oh. This room is starting to move. It's going *up, up, up*.

I don't want to go *up, up, up*. I want to go *down, down, down*.

"Let me out of here!" I bark.

All the two-legs in the room move away from me. But they can't go very far. The room is small.

The two-legs point and shout at Fala and me.

Just then, the doors open. Fala runs out. I follow right behind.

The two-legs leave, too. Some of them are still pointing at me and yelling lots of words. The only words I understand are *no* and *dogs*.

"Sparky! Over here!" Fala calls from the other side of the room.

I run over to Fala and look out the window that he's standing next to. Gulp! The ground looks far, far away. I don't like it up here.

But Fala is happy. He starts pointing with his snout. "See that building with the round roof?" he asks. "That's the Capitol building."

"What's a 'capitol'?" I ask Fala. "Is

it a kind of two-leg? Do all the capitols live in one building?"

Fala laughs, like I've just made a funny joke. He doesn't answer me. Instead he smiles and licks his lips. "One time I found a whole hamburger on those stairs," he tells me. "With ketchup!"

Yum. I would sure like to find a hamburger on the ground right now. Actually, I'd just like to *be* on the ground—instead of all the way up here.

"Another time, a two-leg spilled a box of popcorn," Fala continues. "I had to fight a whole bunch of pigeons, but I got a lot of that popcorn."

I look down at the ground again. We're so high in the sky. Suddenly, my head feels all woozy. My stomach starts flipping and flopping.

"I don't feel so good," I tell Fala.

Blehhhh . . . Suddenly all the chewed-up pretzel pieces go flying out of my mouth.

The two-legs turn and look at me. They use their paws to cover their noses. The two-legs do not look happy. I don't blame them. I'm not happy, either.

"I gotta get out of here," I tell Fala.

"Follow me." Fala turns and starts running down some stairs.

There are two-legs on the stairs. But I don't let them stop me. I keep running, pushing them out of the way.

The two-legs yell as I push past them.

Down. Down. Down.

There are so many stairs. My heart is *thumpety, thump, thumping*. My paws are aching. But I don't stop until I'm outside again.

"Are you okay?" Fala asks me once we are standing outside.

"I am now," I tell him.

Grumble. Rumble.

My tummy starts talking. It's hungry because it's empty now.

Grumble. Rumble. Fala's tummy is talking, too.

"Come on, Sparky," Fala tells me. "Let's go find some food!"

"I'll go anywhere," I tell him. "As long as I get to keep my paws down here on the ground."

The Muffin Shop
The best muffin in Washington

CHAPTER 5

"This is yummy!" I say as I bite into my very first blueberry muffin. "I've never tasted anything like this."

"What did I tell you?" Fala asks. "My two-legs used to go into that muffin shop all the time. I would wait outside. When they came out, they would give me muffin scraps."

"Your two-legs sound nice," I say.

Then I frown. My two-leg, Josh, is nice, too. He was nicer before he found his new friend. But he's still nice. And I bet he would like these muffins.

"They're not my two-legs anymore," Fala corrects me. "I'm a free dog. I don't need two-legs to get muffin scraps. They're not here today, are they? And I'm still eating muffin scraps."

That's funny. Fala should sound happy that there are so many muffins for us. But he doesn't. He sounds a little sad.

Achoo! Fala sneezes, and muffin crumbs splatter all over the place. I laugh.

Fala gives me a weird look, like he doesn't know why I'm laughing. But then he laughs, too. "You're a funny guy, Sparkster. I'm glad we met."

"Me too," I tell him.

Fala looks around. "We're all

out of muffins," he says. "Maybe we should go hang out near the National Air and Space Museum next."

I start to ask Fala what that is. But he doesn't give me a chance. He just keeps talking.

"My two-legs used to take me on walks past the National Air and Space Museum," he says as we start off. "The little two-legs would get pretzels and share them with me. I really loved those little two-legs . . ." Fala stops and shakes his head.

"I mean I love *all* little two-legs, because they drop their food a lot. That's the best. Right, Sparkster?"

I don't think Fala was really talking about food. But I still have to agree with him. Dropped food is great.

"It sure is, Falster," I tell him.

Fala laughs. *Achoo.* And sneezes.

I go to cross the street. Then I stop. And jump back.

Whoosh! A metal machine with four round paws zooms past me. Then another. And another.

My tail flops sadly. I wonder how many of the two-legs in those metal machines have left their dogs home alone with no one to play with.

Maybe Fala's right. Maybe dogs *don't* need two-legs. I kind of like not having anyone around to tell me what to do—or what *not* to do.

But there's no one around to pet me or tell me I'm a good dog, either.

"Okay, Sparky," Fala says a few minutes later. "Here we are. The National Air and Space Museum."

I see a big building with lots of stairs and windows. There's something tall and shiny near the building. On the very top, there are sparkly things that look like the dots that come out when the sun disappears.

"Check out all the little two-legs," Fala tells me.

"I wonder what food they'll drop," I say. "I'm hoping for a hunk of . . ."

But Fala isn't listening to me. He's staring at two young two-legs sitting on a bench, eating pretzels. One is a girl two-leg with long curly fur. The other is a boy. I can't see the fur on *his* head. It's covered up.

Fala's tail starts going crazy. The next thing I know, my friend is running over to the young two-legs. He goes right up to them and sniffs their feet. The girl two-leg laughs. But the boy jumps up and holds his pretzel close.

Fala shakes his head. His tail droops.

"Let's get out of here, Sparky," Fala says sadly as he walks back over to me. "They're not the two-legs I thought . . ."

Fala doesn't finish his sentence. He just shakes his head.

Hmmmm . . . I don't think Fala was looking for pretzel scraps after all. I think he was looking for someone. Or maybe some*ones*.

"Fala?" I ask. "Do you ever miss your two-legs?"

Fala's eyes open wide. He looks surprised. "What kind of question is that?" he barks angrily.

Maybe I better not talk about that anymore. I don't want my new friend to be angry. "Let's go find more scraps," I say. "Maybe pizza crusts."

"Sure, I know where we can get pizza crusts," Fala says. He starts to walk away. But his tail doesn't wag and his mouth doesn't smile. He just looks back at the two-legs on the bench and sneezes.

Achoo.

CHAPTER 6

Toot. Toot. Toot.

There's a lot of tooting coming from under my tail. It happens whenever I eat a hot dog. And Fala and I just finished sharing a whole hot dog that we found next to a tree.

"I haven't eaten a hot dog since the time my two-legs made that fire in our yard and . . . ," Fala begins.

Toot. Toot. Toot.

"Stop tooting!" I bark at the part of me that's under my tail.

Fala laughs.

“Hot dogs sure are yummy,” I say. “I really like the way they . . .”

This time I’m the one who doesn’t finish what he’s saying. That’s because all I can think about is a big shiny stick that’s flying toward me. I don’t know where it came from. I don’t care. I just gotta have that stick!

I leap up in the air, open my mouth, and . . . YES!

Ow. This is not a normal stick. It's cold. And hard. It hurts my teeth when I bite down.

"Good catch!" Fala tells me.

Just then, a girl two-leg runs over. This must be her stick. I drop the stick at her feet and wait for her to throw it again.

The two-leg picks up the stick.

Wiggle, waggle, hooray! This two-leg wants to play.

"Throw it! Throw it!" I bark.

But the two-leg doesn't throw the stick. Instead she walks over to a group of other two-legs. They're also throwing shiny sticks in the air and catching them.

The two-leg who threw the stick to me throws her stick up in the air.

But she doesn't catch it. It falls to the ground.

The other two-legs shake their heads and move away.

The two-leg who dropped the stick looks sad. Water starts dripping from her eyes.

I know why. The other two-legs are playing together. But she's alone. It's no fun playing by yourself.

Achoo! Fala sneezes. "Let's get out of here," he says. "There are too many cherry blossoms. I don't know why two-legs love them so much."

"How do you know they love cherry blossoms?" I ask.

"Why else would they have a parade for them?" Fala replies.

"What's a parade?" I ask him.

"It's like a big two-leg party," Fala says. "They march down the street and make a lot of noise. Some of them throw sticks."

That doesn't sound like much fun. Except for the throwing-sticks part.

"Those girl two-legs are getting ready to throw their sticks up and down in the National Cherry Blossom Festival Parade," Fala tells me. "I don't know why two-legs get so excited about those rotten flowers. All they do is make me sneeze."

Achoo!

I know why the two-legs like the flowers. They're pretty. And they smell nice.

Achoo! Achoo!

But I also know why Fala *doesn't* like them.

"Let's go," Fala says. "There are scraps out there with our names on them!"

"The scraps know our names?" I ask him.

Fala laughs. "I just meant that there are probably a lot of scraps on the ground. We should find them and eat them."

Oh. That makes more sense.

CHAPTER 7

"Hey, you two better get out of here!"

As Fala and I turn a corner, we hear a dog barking at us. I look over and see a dog with black-and-white shaggy fur. He's running around the biggest yard I've ever seen.

The yard is surrounded by a tall fence. The black-and-white dog can't get out. And Fala and I can't get in. But we can all still talk to each other through the fence, the same way I talk to my buddies Frankie the

German shepherd and Samson the mixed-breed dog back home.

I wonder what Samson and Frankie are doing right now. I wonder if they're wondering what *I'm* doing right now.

"You don't want to be here when the Big Guy arrives," the black-and-white dog tells Fala and me.

"Who's the Big Guy?" I ask nervously.

"His two-leg," Fala explains. "Haven't you heard of the Big Guy?"

I shake my head. The only big guy I know is Josh. He's pretty tall. But he's not here.

"Doesn't the Big Guy like dogs?" I ask.

"Sure," the dog behind the fence

says. "He just doesn't like them being off-leash."

"Your two-leg sounds mean," I tell him.

"He's not," the dog behind the fence assures me. "He plays ball with me, and he lets me curl up on the floor under his big desk."

"That does sound nice," I say. "My two-leg . . . ," I begin. But then I stop. I don't know if I'll be able to curl up at Josh's feet anymore. And he sure didn't want to play with me today.

Achoo. Fala sneezes. "Stupid Rose Garden. Roses make me sneeze worse than cherry blossoms." He wipes his nose with his paw.

"The Big Guy thinks dogs should be in their own yards or on leashes," the dog behind the fence continues. "And everyone listens to the Big Guy."

"Cats, too?" I wonder.

The dog behind the fence thinks about that. "Actually, I don't know about cats," he says finally. "They don't really listen to anybody. But if they did, they'd listen to the Big Guy."

I want to say that the Big Guy would like Fala and me if he got to know us, but I don't get the chance. Suddenly the biggest bird I've ever seen flies over the giant green yard.

It sure is a strange bird. It doesn't have wings on the side of its body.

This bird's wings are over the top. And they whirl around and around instead of flapping up and down. This bird doesn't chirp, either. It whirs. Loudly.

The big whirring bird is really scary. And it's just about to land!

Thumpety, thump, thump, thump. My heart is thumping. My tail is drooping. And my paws are starting to bounce. They want to get out of here. Right now.

Before I even know what's happening, my paws start to run. Fast. Faster. *Fastest!*

"Hey, Sparkster! Wait for me!" Fala shouts.

I want to wait for Fala. But I can't. I'm too scared.

Achoo. Fala's running behind me. "Sparky, wait up," he calls to me again.

Screech! This time my paws stop short and wait under a tree for Fala.

"That was one scary bird," I say once Fala catches up to me. "I'm glad we don't have birds like that in my yard."

"My yard is . . . I mean, *was* . . . way too small to fit a bird like that," Fala says.

I look up to make sure there aren't any more giant whirlybirds in the sky. I don't see any. But I do see a piece of paper hanging from a tree.

The paper has a picture of a dog on it, just like the one I saw before.

"Fala, isn't that you?" I ask him.

Fala cocks his head. He looks at the picture. Then he says, “That could be any dog. There are lots of terriers in this town. Why would my picture be hanging from a tree, anyway?”

I don’t know why. I just know the dog on the paper looks like Fala.

Fala starts walking down the street. I follow close behind. While we walk, I think about how lucky the dog behind the fence is, because he has the Big Guy to play with. It's nice to have a two-leg to play with.

I wish I had my two-leg to play with. I sure miss Josh.

CHAPTER 8

"Aahhh . . . This is the life," Fala says a little while later. "There's nothing better than a peanut-butter sandwich with hardly any dirt on it. Yum."

I swallow a big bite of peanut butter and bread. Then I roll over and scratch my back on the steps of the Capitol building.

I know it's the Capitol building because Fala showed it to me before, when we were way up high in the sky.

"The people who work in the

Capitol building bring the best lunches," Fala tells me.

"How do you know that?" I ask him.

"One of the two-legs I used to live with came here every day," he tells me. "Sometimes the other two-legs in my family would bring me here so I could play with her while she ate lunch."

Fala sounds happy when he talks about his two-legs, which is weird, because he keeps telling me how happy he is without them.

I wonder if the family Fala used to live with still thinks about him.

I wonder if Josh is thinking about *me*.

Suddenly, Fala's tail starts to

wag. His ears perk up. His paws start moving toward a two-leg with curly yellow fur on her head. She's walking up the stairs.

I don't know what's so exciting about that two-leg. She's not throwing a ball or holding food.

Still Fala is zooming after her.

"Hey, Fala! Wait for me!" I bark as I run after him.

But my friend doesn't wait. He keeps running. And so do I.

The next thing I know, Fala and I are inside the Capitol building!

The two-leg turns around and looks at us. Her eyes open wide. She scratches her curly yellow fur, and says something to another two-leg who is standing near the door.

I don't know what she's saying. But I can tell when someone is trying to catch me. And that's what the two-leg near the door is trying to do. He's running right toward Fala and me, with his arms out.

"Run, Fala, run!" I bark.

Fala looks back at the two-leg woman. His tail isn't wagging anymore. He doesn't look happy.

I don't blame him. You can't be happy when you're about to get caught!

"Run, Fala, run!" I bark again.

This time Fala runs. So do I. We run right into a big round room filled with two-leg statues—and a whole group of *real* two-legs, too.

The statues don't care about Fala and me. But the real two-legs do. They're yelling and pointing.

"Run, Sparky!" Fala barks.

He doesn't have to tell me twice. My paws already are on the move. They're running. Fast. Faster. *Fastest.*

My fur flies in my eyes. I can't see where I'm going. But I can hear Fala's

paws on the ground.

Achoo! I can hear him sneezing.

"Right behind you!" I bark.

I shake my head hard, to try to get the fur out of my eyes. But the shaking doesn't work.

"Bad fur!" I bark. "Let me see."

My eyes may be covered, but my ears aren't. I hear a whole lot of two-legs. They're yelling. But they don't seem to be yelling at me. I haven't heard the words *no* or *bad dog*. Not even once.

I stop and shake my head. This time the fur moves away from my eyes. *Wiggle, waggle, whoopee!* I can see.

What I see surprises me. The two-legs aren't yelling at me. They're yelling at each other. They're so angry, they don't even notice that Fala and I are there.

"Over here, Sparky," Fala barks to me.

Fala is on the other side of the room. To reach him, I will have to run through a row of two-legs. What if one of them grabs me?

I can't stay here. I gotta take the chance.

Quickly, I run right through the row of two-legs. One by one, they leap out of their chairs. I guess they're surprised to feel a furry puppy running past them.

The two-legs are still yelling. But now they're yelling at me. I hear the words *dog* and *no*.

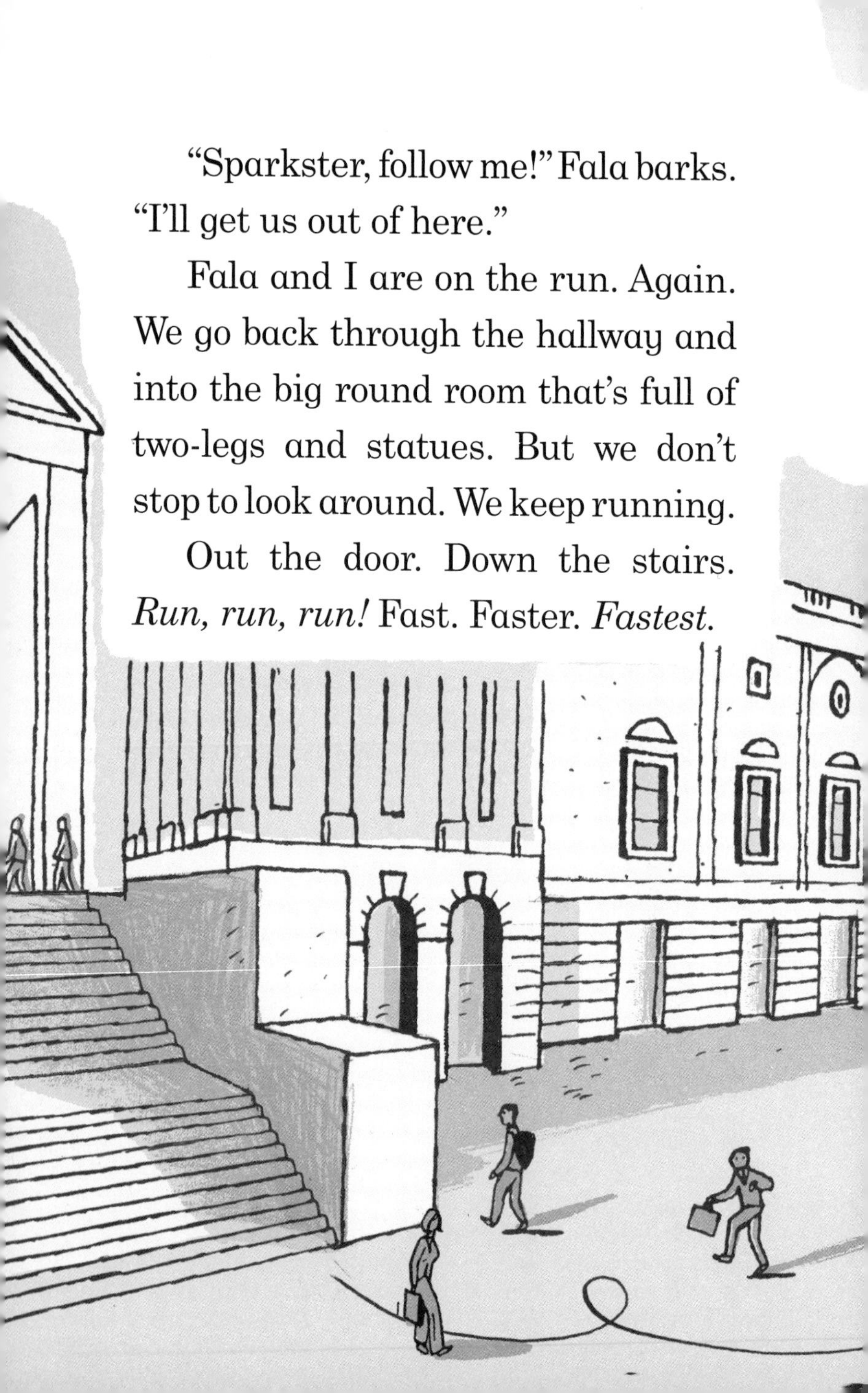

"Sparkster, follow me!" Fala barks. "I'll get us out of here."

Fala and I are on the run. Again. We go back through the hallway and into the big round room that's full of two-legs and statues. But we don't stop to look around. We keep running.

Out the door. Down the stairs. *Run, run, run!* Fast. Faster. *Fastest.*

CHAPTER 9

Fala and I don't stop running until we're far away from the Capitol.

"Boy, those two-legs were angry with us," I say, finally.

"They were angry before we got there," Fala says. "Didn't you hear them?" He sneezes. *Achoo.*

"What were they doing?" I ask him.

"The people in the Capitol building make laws," Fala explains. "So I guess they were making laws."

"What are laws?" I ask.

"They're like rules," Fala explains.

I know what rules are. Josh has lots of rules: No eating food from the table. No chewing shoes. No burying my toys in the couch cushions.

I *miss* those rules. I miss Josh.

Fala and I turn a corner, and I see lots and lots of two-legs.

"It's the National Cherry Blossom Festival Parade!" Fala announces. *Achoo.*

"Look! There are the two-leg girls with the hard sticks!" I tell Fala.

The two-leg girls are walking past us. They are throwing their sticks high in the air and catching them.

The sticks go up. The sticks go down. Up and down. Up and down.

I love catching sticks. I want to catch a stick. *I GOTTA CATCH A STICK!*

I hurry over to the two-leg I saw before. Maybe she will play with me. Yay! She's throwing her stick in the air. I think she wants me to catch it.

I jump up in the air, with my mouth wide open. Here comes the stick. It's heading for me. It's . . .

Rats! She caught that stick in her paw before I could get to it.

The girl two-leg has a big smile on her face. No wonder she's happy. I'm always happy when I catch a stick.

"You'll get it next time," Fala says as he hurries to catch up to me.

The two-leg throws her stick back into the air. She twirls around, reaches up her hands . . .

Achoo! Just then Fala lets out a big sneeze.

The two-leg looks down at him for just a

second, and . . . *CLANG*. The stick drops to the ground. The two-leg girl looks sad. Water starts to drip from her eyes.

"Don't be sad, two-leg," I bark. I grab the stick with my mouth and hold it up for her.

She takes the stick from me and throws it into the air.

This time, I twirl around and catch the stick in my mouth. That's one of my best tricks. Josh taught me how to do it.

The two-legs in the crowd shout. But they sound happy, not angry. I think they liked my trick!

The water stops dripping from the two-leg's eyes. She smiles and takes the stick from my mouth. She throws it in the air. I twirl around and catch it again.

The other two-legs with sticks smile at her. I'm glad to know she has friends. Friends are important.

"Come on, Fala!" I bark to *my* friend. "You can play, too."

Fala watches as a different two-leg girl throws a stick in the air. He leaps up and catches it in his mouth. The two-legs in the crowd shout happily again.

The two-leg girl takes the stick

from Fala's mouth. She picks him up as the crowd dances by.

"Isn't fetch the best?" I shout to Fala.

But Fala doesn't answer. He isn't interested in fetch. He's too busy staring into the crowd of two-legs.

Huh? That doesn't make any sense. What could possibly be more interesting than playing fetch?

CHAPTER 10

"There they are!" Fala barks excitedly. "All of them."

My friend has a big smile on his face. His tail is wagging like crazy.

"All *who* are?" I start to ask him. I stand on my hind legs and raise my head high. I am trying to see whom Fala is talking about.

He's staring at a family of two-legs. They're standing right near a big blue box.

The tallest one is chubby, and he's missing some of the fur on his head.

The next tallest one is a lady two-leg with yellow fur. Next to them are two younger two-legs: a girl with long curly fur, and a boy whose fur I can't see because it's covered up.

I think I've seen those two-legs before. I look again. No, I haven't seen those exact two-legs. But I have seen two-legs who look a lot like them—at the National Mall, outside the National Air and Space Museum, and at the Capitol building.

Wait a minute. Those were all the places where Fala tried to get scraps from two-legs. *Unless* . . .

Maybe scraps weren't what Fala was looking for after all. Maybe he took me to places where his two-legs used to take him *because he was looking for his family.*

"That's them!" Fala barks. "Those are my two-legs."

I guess I'm not the only one who has been missing his family.

"Let me down!" Fala barks to the two-leg who is holding him. "I have to go to my family."

But the two-leg who is holding Fala doesn't speak dog. She keeps walking.

I take a quick look. The blue box is getting farther and farther away as I walk alongside the two-legs with the sticks.

"Jump down!" I bark to Fala.

"From up here?" Fala looks down. "Are you crazy? It's too high."

Fala is scared to be up high?

Wiggle, waggle, weird. He wasn't scared to be up high at the Washington Monument.

Fala *has* to jump down if he's ever going to see his family again. I have to help him. Just like he's been helping me all day. But how?

Come on, Sparky, I tell myself. *Thinkety, think, think.*

Just then I see a big stick with pink flowers lying on the ground. Hmmm. I wonder if the two-leg girl is allergic like Fala is.

There's only one way to find out. I grab the flowery stick in my teeth and wave it under her nose.

AACHOOOOO!

The two-leg girl sneezes hard.

Achoo! Fala sneezes hard.

The two-leg girl lets go of Fala and wipes her nose with her paw.

Whoa! Fala falls.

Ouch! Fala lands right on top of me. It hurts a little. But not too bad. Fala isn't very big.

"Come on!" I say as he scrambles off me. "Let's find your two-legs."

"I don't know where they are," Fala barks nervously. He doesn't sound brave and fun anymore. He sounds scared and sad.

But he shouldn't be. Because I know where his family is. Right near the big blue box.

But where is the big blue box?

From where I'm standing, all I see are legs. Big legs. Small legs. Thin legs. Fat legs. Lots and lots of legs.

I look between all the legs. Finally, I spot the big blue box.

"Follow me!" I bark.

I run between the two-legs. They jump out of the way when they see me coming.

I keep my eye on the blue box. I don't even turn around to see if Fala is behind me.

Achoo.

I don't have to. I can hear him.

"There they are!" Fala barks.

The next thing I know, he's leaping up into the air.

The chubby two-leg with the fur missing from the top of his head catches him. His eyes open wide. Fala's tail wags wildly.

"Fala! Fala!" the younger two-legs shout.

"It's me!" Fala barks back. "It's me!"

Fala sounds happy. His two-legs sound happy, too. Fala is going home.

I think it's time for me to go home, too. I turn and start to leave.

"Hey, Sparky!" Fala calls to me. "You don't have to go. You can come home with us."

I shake my head. Fala's family isn't my family. *Josh* is my family.

"Thanks for everything," I tell Fala. "But I've gotta go."

CHAPTER 11

Diggety, dig, dig.

I'm back at the National Mall, digging up my bone. I'm glad Fala found his family. He sure looked happy to be back with them. And they sure looked happy to have him back.

I hope Josh feels the same way about me. Because a dog needs a two-leg to love him. And a two-leg needs a dog to love him, too.

Diggety, dig, dig. My bone! It smells just as *yummy, yum, yum* as it did before I buried it in this hole. It's time for me to take a big bite.

But wait. What's that on the ground? It's a stick with a piece of paper hanging from it. Maybe if I bring this stick back to Josh, he and I can play fetch with it.

I go over and grab the stick with the paper hanging from it. Then I walk back to my bone. I open my mouth. And . . .

CHOMP!

Wiggle, waggle, whew. I feel dizzy—like my insides are spinning all around—but my outsides are standing still. Stars are twinkling in front of my eyes, even though it's daytime! All around me I smell food—fried chicken, salmon, roast beef. But there isn't any food in sight.

Kaboom! Kaboom! Kaboom!

The *kabooming* stops. I'm back in my yard. But my yard isn't sunny and bright like it was this morning. Soon it will be dark. The sun is going to sleep.

I want to go to sleep, too. But I can't. I have to bury my bone and keep it safe.

Diggety, dig, dig. I dig a big hole by the flower bed. I drop my bone in the hole and push the dirt back over it.

Now I need to go into the house to look for Josh. I scoot through my doggie door to take a look.

First I check the kitchen.

No Josh.

Maybe he's on the couch in the living room.

Nope. No Josh here, either.

My heart starts *thumpety, thump, thumping.* What if Josh is gone forever? What if he went to live with his new friend? What if I'm going to be alone, always?

Suddenly I hear a metal machine with four round paws. It stops outside my house. I leap onto the couch. I look out the window.

Josh is home! And he's walking toward the gate that leads to our backyard.

I zoom into the kitchen and out to the yard through my doggie door.

"Hi, Josh!" I bark as the gate swings open.

"Sparky!" Josh shouts.

Josh is holding some papers in his hands. But he drops them on the ground when he runs toward me. The papers have a picture of a dog on them. The dog looks a lot like me. I wonder what Josh was going to do with all those pictures.

But Josh doesn't seem to care about the pictures now. He's too busy scratching me behind the ears. *Scratchity, scratch, scratch.*

Josh's scratching can mean only one thing—he still loves me! *Wiggle, waggle, woo-hoo!*

I look around for Josh's new friend, but I don't see her anywhere. Which means that it's just Josh and me.

Josh looks down at the ground. He sees the stick I brought home. He picks it up and looks at it funny.

I wish I could tell Josh where I found the stick. I wish I could tell him about the National Mall, the big statue sitting in a chair, the dog that lives behind a fence with the

Big Guy, and about Fala, who sneezes all the time. But I can't.

So I try to tell him something else. "Throw the stick!" I bark. "Throw the stick."

I don't think Josh understands, because he doesn't throw the stick. Instead, he puts it in his pocket, with the paper sticking out. *Boo*. That's no fun.

Josh bends down and picks up a ball. He tosses it across the yard.

"Fetch, Sparky!"

I know what that means. I zoom across the yard and scoop up the ball in my mouth. I run back to Josh and drop it at his feet.

Josh picks up the ball and throws it again. He's playing with me. *Just with me.*

I guess Josh has to have some two-leg friends. Just like I have some dog friends.

But that doesn't change anything. He will always be my Josh. And I will always be his Sparky. After all, we're a family.

Fun Facts about Sparky's Adventures in Washington, DC

The Lincoln Memorial

The Lincoln Memorial was built in 1914 to honor the sixteenth president of the United States, Abraham Lincoln. In the center of the building is a statue of President Lincoln that stands nineteen feet tall, which is about the height of three grown men standing on one another's shoulders.

The National Mall

Every year more than twenty-four million people visit this park in downtown Washington, DC. Spanning over a thousand acres, this park extends from the Washington Monument to the United States Capitol. The tree-lined park has been used as a place for peaceful protests, concerts, and festivals. It is also a great place to go for a run or have a picnic.

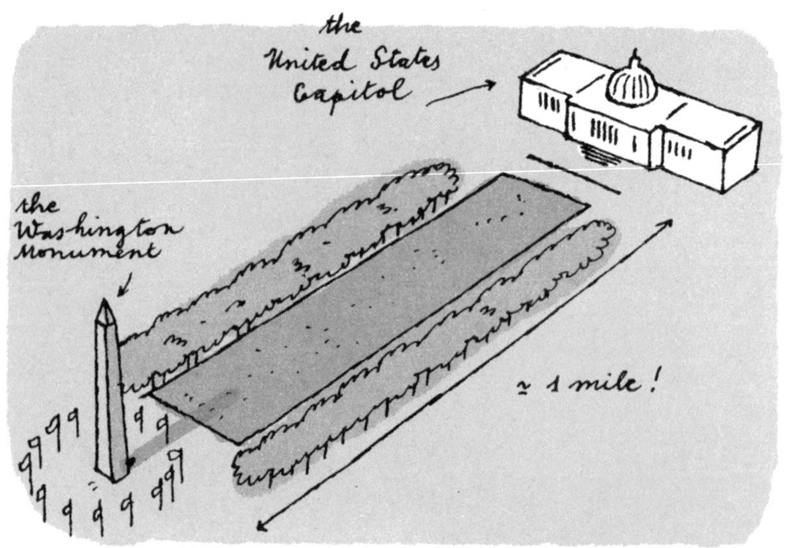

The Washington Monument

The Washington Monument is dedicated to George Washington, the first American president and leader of the Continental Army. The mostly marble building stands 555 feet high! That makes it one of the tallest stone buildings in the world. There are 897 steps leading to the top of the monument, but most visitors take the elevator.

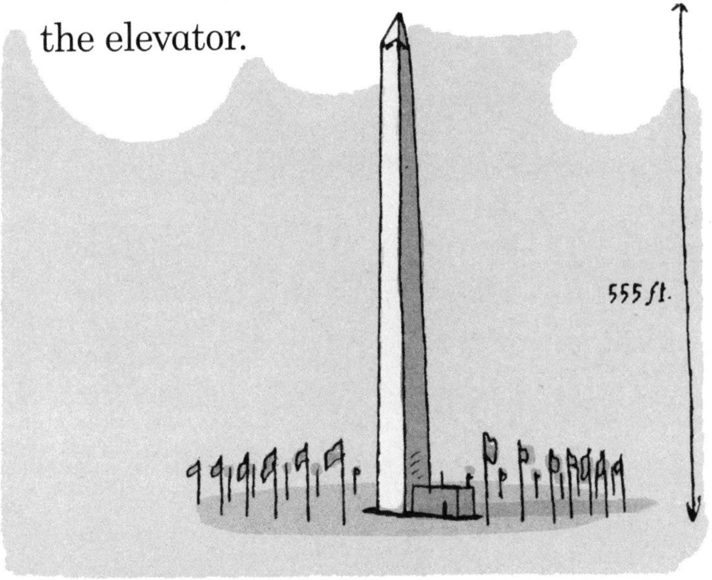

555 ft.

The Smithsonian National Air and Space Museum

The National Air and Space Museum is part of the Washington, DC, Smithsonian Institution, which includes nineteen different museums and art galleries and the National Zoo. Visitors to the National Air and Space Museum can see the 1903 *Wright Flyer*, the first heavier-than-air plane to fly. They can also see the Apollo 11 Command Module, which carried US astronauts to the moon for the first time. The stainless-steel sculpture outside the museum is called *Ad Astra*, which means *to the stars*.

The White House

Home to the president of the United States, the White House has 132 rooms, including a bowling alley and a movie theater. Over the years, the White House has been home to lots of presidential pets. Many have been dogs and cats, but there have been more unusual animals, like John Quincy Adams's alligator (which he kept in a bathtub!), Abraham Lincoln's goat and turkey, Martin Van Buren's two tiger cubs, and the flock of sheep Woodrow Wilson kept on the White House lawn to keep the grass trimmed!

The United States Capitol

The United States Capitol is where the members of the US Congress work. The US Congress, which makes the laws that govern the United States, has two houses, or parts—the House of Representatives and the Senate. The Capitol has a big dome in the center and two wings—one for each house of Congress. The Senate chamber was completed in 1800, and the House chamber in 1807.

The National Cherry Blossom Festival Parade®

Each spring, this festival celebrates the 1912 gift of 3,000 cherry trees from the mayor of Tokyo, Japan, to the city of Washington, DC.

About the Author

Nancy Krulik is the author of more than 200 books for children and young adults, including three *New York Times* Best Sellers. She is best known for being the author and creator of several successful book series for children, including Katie Kazoo, Switcheroo; How I Survived Middle School; and George Brown, Class Clown. Nancy lives in Manhattan with her husband, composer Daniel Burwasser, and her crazy beagle mix, Josie, who manages to drag her along on many exciting adventures without ever leaving Central Park.

About the Illustrator

You could fill a whole attic with Seb's drawings! His collection includes some very early pieces made when he was four—there is even a series of drawings he did at the movies in the dark! When he isn't doodling, he likes to make toys and sculptures, as well as bows and arrows for his two boys, Oscar and Leo, and their numerous friends. Seb is French and lives in England. His website is www.sebastienbraun.com.